W9-BMT-953

Kitty Dreams

Vanita   In memory of Evelyn, who would have loved cats just like her mommy and daddy, and to all my other grandchildren.

Kristin   For all the wonderful cats I know. To George, Martha, Oreo, Peaches, Brutus, Sasha, Mackenzie, Tess, Rico, Zebee, Kitifer, Otis, Minky, and Maude.

Acknowledgments   Kristin Blackwood, Mike Blanc, Sheila Tarr, Michael Olin-Hitt, Kurt Landefeld, Paul Royer, Jennie Levy Smith, Cinda Dehner, and Gailmarie Fort

VanitaBooks, LLC

Carrot
VanitaBooks, LLC
All Rights Reserved. ©2011 by Vanita Oelschlager.

No part of this book may be reproduced, stored in or introduced into a retrieval system, or transmitted, in any form or by any means (electronic, mechanical, photocopying, recording or any other system currently known or yet to be invented) – except by reviewers, who may quote brief passages in a review to be printed in a newspaper or print or online publication – without the express written permission of both the author and the illustrator, as well as the copyright owner of this book, Vanita Oelschlager. The scanning, uploading, and distribution of this book via the Internet or via any other means without the prior permission of the publisher is illegal and punishable by law. Please do not participate in or encourage electronic piracy of copyrighted materials. Your support of the author's and illustrator's rights is appreciated.

Text by Vanita Oelschlager
Illustrations by Kristin Blackwood

Printed in China.
Hardcover Edition ISBN 978-0-9819714-9-0
Paperback Edition ISBN 978-0-9826366-0-2

www.VanitaBooks.com

Carrot

Story by
Vanita Oelschlager

Illustrations by
Kristin Blackwood

Carrot was a cat

content day to day.

She would nap until noon,

then head out to play.

Her name was Carrot

because of her coat.

It was orange like a life jacket

hung on a boat.

Carrot spent some time

with her family each day.

She was always underfoot,

but not in the way.

Carrot lived in a house

not too big, not too small.

In a city of buildings,

some short and some tall.

She would walk through the city

spring, summer and fall.

She'd talk to the alley cat

if he gave her a call.

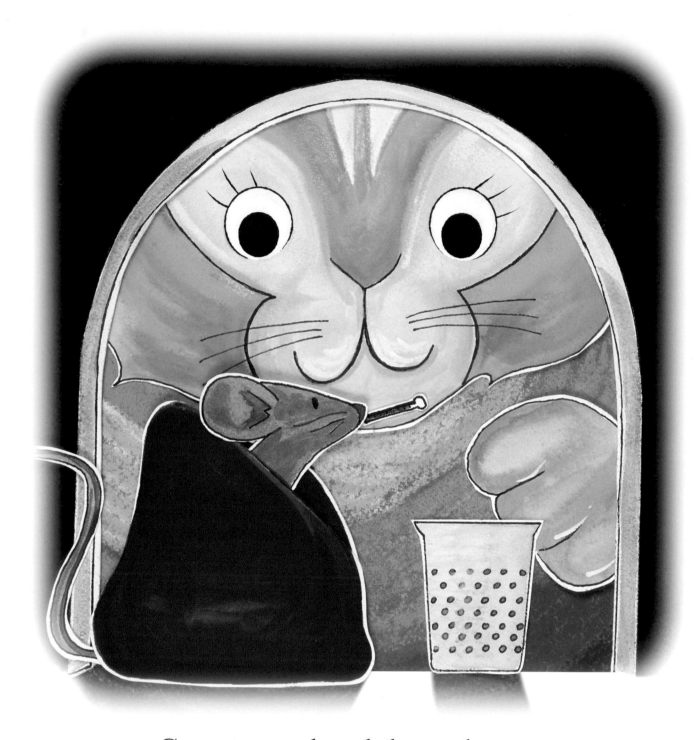

Carrot wandered through town,

being kind to all she knew.

She was once seen taking soup

to a mouse with the flu.

She would chase mice down Broadway

and then up to Main.

But she usually lost them,

all that chasing in vain.

She would often stop off

at Finney's great diner.

No morsel of food

could taste any finer.

This was the life,

each day in the city.

There could be nothing better

for this down-to-earth kitty.

One day Carrot woke up

from her fifth nap of the day.

She wandered outside

and down to the bay.

On a fancy boat,

called a yacht at the pier

she saw a lovely cat

with a bow on one ear.

She was beautiful to see,

pure white and all fluffy.

And a woman in chiffon

was calling her Buffy.

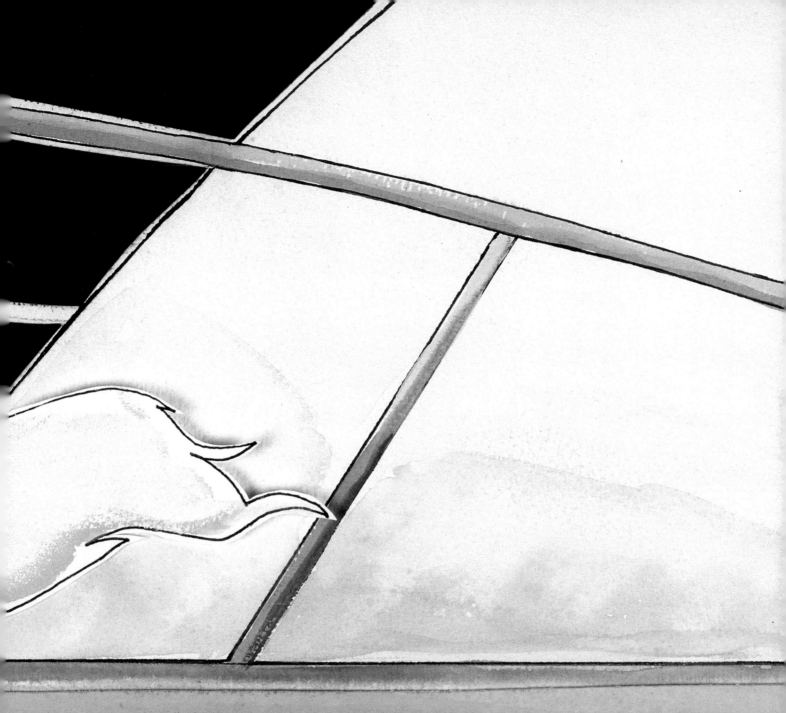

Her collar was gleaming

in the bright midday sun.

And she batted a toy mouse

around just for fun.

This cat on the yacht

seemed like she had it all,

with her own pile of pillows,

nearly 20 feet tall.

This cat was like nothing

Carrot had ever seen.

She must have been born

of a king and a queen.

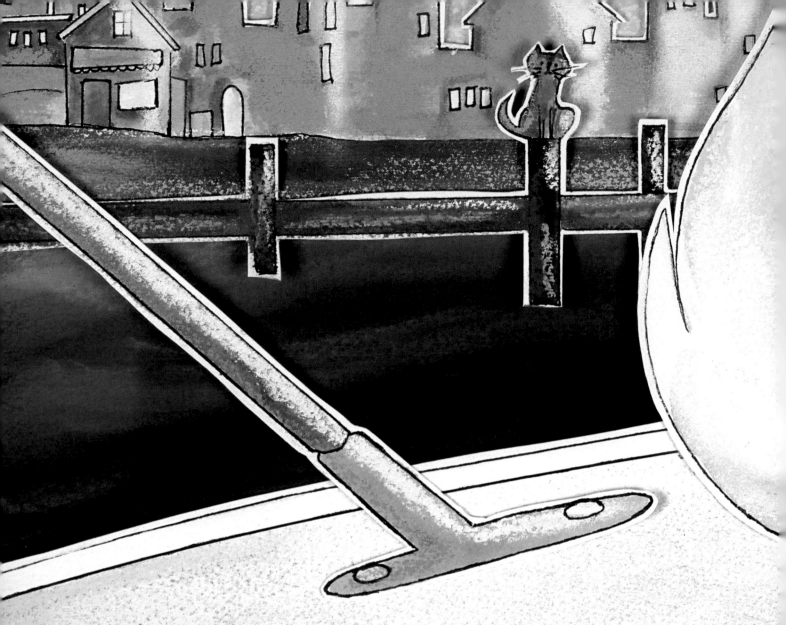

It was hard for Carrot

to take her eyes off this creature.

Carrot studied Buffy's

every graceful white feature.

Carrot wondered what it'd be like

to live for a day,

the life of that cat

she'd seen down by the bay.

Later that night

when Carrot got home,

she dreamt of that cat

high up on her throne.

Every nap would be long

and the absolute best.

All in the name

of a good beauty rest.

She would dine every night

on the finest caviar.

Anything that she wished for

was never too far.

Carrot would have a collar

of diamonds and pearls.

She would have tea every day

at three with the girls.

If Carrot were that cat,

she'd have her own plane.

Stocked with only the best

milk-flavored champagne.

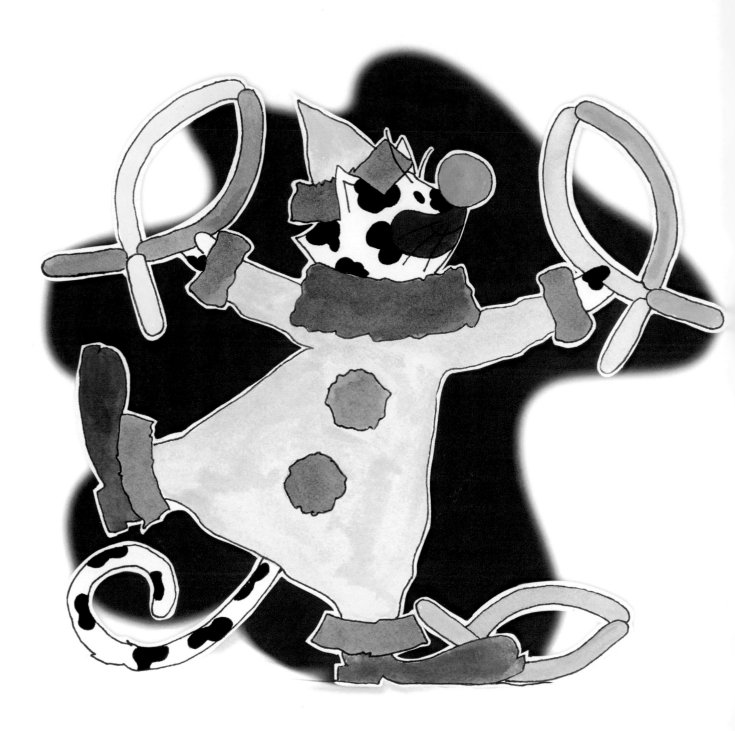

There would be servants galore

to fill every wish,

and a clown named Loomis

making balloons into fish.

She could have a party,

a kitty cotillion.

Full of rich socialites

from a town called Vermilion.

She would be asked to marry

the Earl of Kent's cat.

Nothing could be

more romantic than that.

Yes, a life like Buffy's

would seem like a dream.

But maybe it wasn't

as great as it seemed.

Maybe diamonds were nice;

Carrot thought that they were.

But keeping her looks

could be hard on her fur.

No real mice were ever

found on their yacht.

So Buffy played with a toy

that always stayed caught.

Tuna for breakfast

would be a fancy affair,

but bratwurst from Finney's

on a yacht would be rare.

Buffy had very few friends

because of her travels.

This luxury cat's life

began to unravel.

The cat on the yacht

was not so different than she.

All cats have good and bad

on land or on sea.

Carrot's house was not big,

but also not small.

It started to look

not too bad at all.

Without their sweet Carrot,

what would her poor family do?

And what of the mouse?

Who would tend to his flu?

The city with its buildings,

some short and some tall

would surely miss her,

if she weren't there at all.

Yes, it might be nice

to be Buffy for a day.

But Carrot could never

live her whole life that way.

She should be a cat's cat,

content day to day,

loving the life that she had.

She was happier that way.

The Author and Artist

Vanita Oelschlager is a wife, mother, grandmother, philanthropist, former teacher, current caregiver, author and poet. A graduate of Mount Union College in Alliance, Ohio, she now serves as a Trustee of her alma mater and as Writer in Residence for the Literacy Program at The University of Akron. Vanita and her husband Jim were honored with a *Lifetime Achievement Award* from the National Multiple Sclerosis Society in 2006. She was the Congressional *Angels in Adoption* award recipient for the State of Ohio in 2007 and was named *National Volunteer of the Year* by the MS Society in 2008. Vanita was also honored in 2009 as the *Woman Philanthropist of the Year* by the Summit County Chapter of the United Way.

Kristin Blackwood is a teacher and frequent illustrator of books for children. Her works of art are published in: *My Grampy Can't Walk*, *Let Me Bee*, *What Pet Will I Get?*, *Made in China*, *Big Blue*, *Ivy in Bloom*, *Ivan's Great Fall*, *A Tale of Two Daddies* and *Bonyo Bonyo*. A graduate of Kent State University, Kristin has a degree in Art History. When she isn't designing or teaching, she enjoys being a mother to her two daughters.

Net Profits

All net profits from this book will be donated to charitable organizations, with a gentle preference toward those serving people with my husband's disease – multiple sclerosis.